WITHDRAWN

Doodleville

DREW
3 YEARS OLD

5 YEARS OLD

7 YEARS OLD

DREW, WE **LOVE** HAVING YOU AT THE DINER ALL THE TIME, BUT...

DON'T YOU WANT TO GO OUT AND **PLAY** MORE?

DON'T YOU WANT TO MAKE **FRIENDS**?

I **HAVE** FRIENDS.

THEY'RE RIGHT **HERE**.

eville

CHAD SELL

ALFRED A. KNOPF ✷ NEW YORK

DREW
NOW

9

10

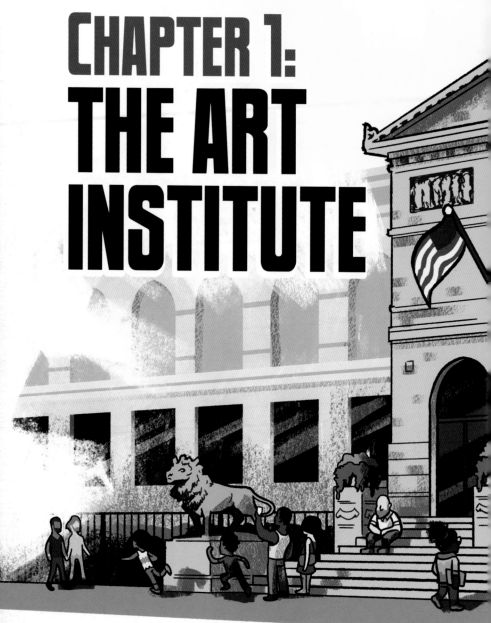

CHAPTER 1: THE ART INSTITUTE

DREW?

DID YOU GET THEM?

IS EVERYTHING OKAY?

WHAT HAPPENED?

CHAPTER 2:
TROUBLE

45

CHAPTER 3: THE WILD WEEK

COOL! SO HE'LL FLY AROUND AND DEFEAT **ALL** THE EVIL?

YEAH! **NOBODY** CAN BEAT CAPTAIN COCKATOO!

YEAH...

WHAT? YOU DON'T **THINK** SO?

I MEAN...

WHO DOES HE ACTUALLY **FIGHT?**

I HAVEN'T EVER SEEN HIM **DO** MUCH...

BESIDES **POSE** LIKE HE'S ON THE COVER OF A COMIC BOOK.

WELL, HE'S **TRAINING!** SO THAT HE'LL BE **READY!**

I JUST NEED TO COME UP WITH A **VILLAIN** FOR HIM TO FIGHT.

A...WORTHY OPPONENT!

THEN HE'LL LEAP INTO ACTION AND **TOTALLY** SAVE THE DAY!

57

I'M SO SORRY, EVERYONE!

BUT... THAT **WAS** KIND OF COOL, RIGHT?

DREW, I THINK WE SHOULD GATHER OUR WORK AND WRAP THINGS UP, OKAY?

RIGHT, OKAY.

TO BE HONEST, I'VE NEVER SEEN CAP MOVE SO FAST!

IT'S ALL GOOD, DREW!

THANKS, AMEER.

I GUESS DINAH DARE GOT A CHANCE TO TEST THAT FORCE FIELD, HUH, BECK?

SO...THAT'S GOOD, RIGHT?

STUPENDOUS.

CHAPTER 4:
THE LEVIATHAN

84

CHAPTER 5: THE DARK LEVIATHAN

LEVI!

LEVI!

ARE YOU OUT THERE?

LEEEEEEVIIIII!!!

I'M SORRY.

...IT WASN'T YOUR **FAULT**.

99

BUT...

BUT IF ANY OF THEM GET **HURT,** I DON'T...

IT WOULD BE ALL MY FAULT.

DREW, STOP...

ALL OF THIS, IT'S...

...IT'S ALL MY FAULT!

DREW!

SERIOUSLY! **STOP!!!!**

123

CHAPTER 6: IN PIECES

I DON'T WANT TO TALK ABOUT IT.

DREW?

SWEETHEART?

BUT, DREW... WE'RE **WORRIED** ABOUT YOU.

YOU CAN **TALK** TO US ABOUT... **WHATEVER** THIS IS.

YOU'RE NOT **EATING**...

NOT **TALKING**...

AND... **WHERE** ARE ALL YOUR DOODLES?

DOODLEVILLE IS **TORN UP** ON THE **FLOOR**...

SWEETHEART, IT'S NOT YOUR FAULT.
BUT IT IS.
I MADE THAT MONSTER, AND NOW NOTHING CAN STOP HIM.
IT'S MY FAULT HE DESTROYED DOODLEVILLE,
AND IT'S MY FAULT THAT HE...
THAT...
DREW? WHAT DID HE DO?
HE KILLED ZENOBIA'S BUTTERFLY PRINCE...
AND I DON'T KNOW IF SHE'LL EVER FORGIVE ME.

WELL...

YOU CAN FIND OUT **SOON**, BECAUSE...

SHE'S **DOWNSTAIRS** IN THE **DINER**.

WHAT?!?

SHE'S **HERE?**

BUT...

I CAN'T.

I DON'T...

I DON'T EVEN KNOW WHAT TO **SAY**.

I THINK YOU KNOW WHERE TO **START**.

BUT...

ZEN, I'M...
I'M **SO**
SORRY.

DREW!

WHY ARE
YOU SORRY?

BECAUSE...

IT'S **MY** FAULT
YOUR PRINCE
IS **DEAD**.

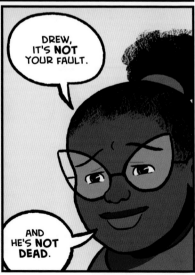

DREW,
IT'S **NOT**
YOUR FAULT.

AND
HE'S **NOT**
DEAD.

BUT...

YOU WERE **THERE**.

YOU **SAW** WHAT HAPPENED.

THE PRINCES ARE MAGICALLY **LINKED**.

IF ONE **DIES**, THE OTHER WILL **KNOW**.

HE'S STILL **INSIDE** THAT THING...

AND WE'RE GONNA GET HIM **BACK**.

WHAT? **WHO** IS?

YOU, ME, OUR FRIENDS.

THE DOODLES. **EVERYONE**.

IT'S TOO **DANGEROUS**, ZEN.

WE CAN'T **BEAT** THE LEVIATHAN.

I THINK YOU'RE **WRONG**, DREW.

BECAUSE **TOGETHER**...

I **THINK** WE CAN DO JUST ABOUT **ANYTHING**.

ZEN TAUGHT THE DOODLES HER BUTTERFLY MAGIC!

AND THEY CAN **LINK** THEIR MAGIC TOGETHER!

AMAZING, RIGHT?

IF SHE COULD DO **THAT**, THEN...

MAYBE ALL OF **YOU** CAN TRAIN THE DOODLES TO BE HEROES, TOO!

BUT...

WE **HAVE** TO WORK TOGETHER, RIGHT?

IT'S, LIKE, THE ENTIRE **POINT** OF THE PLAN.

RIGHT.

BUT NOT UNTIL WE'RE **READY** TO FACE THE LEVIATHAN AGAIN.

UNTIL THEN... WE HAVE TO KEEP THE DOODLES **SAFE**.

YOU HAVE TO KEEP THEM SAFE.

SO, UM... WHO'S FREE AFTER SCHOOL?

SO, DOODLES, HOW ARE YOU FEELING?

WELL, **THEY** SEEM CONFIDENT, BUT...

DO YOU REALLY THINK WE'LL HAVE A **CHANCE** AGAINST THAT...

THE DARK LEVIATHAN?

OF COURSE!

LOOK AT EVERYTHING YOU'VE DONE WITH THE DOODLES ALREADY!

THEY'RE GOING TO BE **AMAZING!**

I **HOPE** SO. I DON'T KNOW WHAT **I'LL** DO WHEN I SEE THAT THING AGAIN.

WELL, IT'S LIKE YOU SAID...

EVERY HERO NEEDS A **"WORTHY OPPONENT,"** RIGHT?

I THINK YOU'VE **FOUND** HIM.

CHAPTER 8: EVIL BAD SCARY STUFF

HI, MOM.

HI, DAD.

GOOD MORNING, SWEETHEART!

GOOD MORNING, DREW!

DREEEW!

HEY, DREW.

HI-- TJ?

WHAT ARE **YOU** DOING HERE?

I CAME WITH ABUELO ERNESTO SO THAT I COULD SHOW YOU SOMETHING.

IS THAT COOL?

OH, SURE...

159

I MEAN...

I'M HAPPY THAT EVERYONE IN ART CLUB IS **HELPING** BUT...

I JUST... I MISS THE **DOODLES**, AND...

I WISH THEY WERE **SAFE** WITH **ME**.

I JUST FEEL LIKE EVERYTHING I DO IS A **DISASTER**.

I KNOW IT MIGHT **FEEL** LIKE THAT,

BUT WE'RE **HERE** FOR YOU. WE'LL FIGURE IT OUT.

THANKS.

YOU'RE BEING NICE.

I SORT OF THOUGHT YOU **HATED** ME.

OOOOH!

ARE YOU TEACHING THEM MAGIC?

BLACK MAGIC?

EVIL BAD **SCARY** STUFF?

YOU'RE NOT A WITCH, ARE YOU?

HAHAHA!

WOULD YOU **TELL** ME IF YOU WERE??

I'M **NOT** A WITCH.

I JUST **LIKE** THAT KINDA STUFF.

WITCHCRAFT?

CURSES AND INCANTATIONS?

NOT EXACTLY...

MORE LIKE... THE **IDEA**.

THAT BEING DIFFERENT CAN MAKE YOU **POWERFUL**.

164

THAT NIGHT...

RR

LEVIATHAN?

IS THAT YOU?

GRRRRR...

SHHH, IT'S OKAY.

174

176

NO, I WAS THINKING ABOUT HOW HE **WAS**, AT FIRST.

WHAT DO YOU MEAN?

HE WAS... **SWEET**.

HE ONLY **ACTED** BAD BECAUSE I WAS **FEELING** BAD.

WE DON'T **BLAME** YOU, DREW.

WE'LL HELP YOU **STOP** HIM.

BUT...

WHAT IF I COULD **SAVE** HIM INSTEAD?

DREW...

THE **PLAN** IS TO DEFEND THE DOODLES AND **SAVE** THE BUTTERFLY PRINCE.

NOT THE MONSTER YOU MADE.

BUT... HE'S A **PART** OF ME!

A PART OF YOU THAT WANTED TO **DESTROY** DOODLEVILLE AND EVERYONE IN IT?

THAT'S NOT FAIR.

I'M SORRY, BUT IT'S **TRUE!**

I'VE GOTTA GO.

DREW, I JUST...

I DON'T WANT YOU TO...

...TO DO SOMETHING **STUPID?**

WELL...

TOO LATE.

180

THAT NIGHT...

HOW ARE YOU, SWEETIE?

ARE YOU **HUNGRY?**

NO...

THEN WHY ARE YOU **DRAWING** SO MUCH FOOD?

IT'S...FOR THE LEVIATHAN.

OH.

I'M...

I WANT TO UNDERSTAND HIM.

MAYBE EVEN **MAKE PEACE** WITH HIM.

ARE YOU... **SURE THAT'S POSSIBLE?**

NOT AT ALL.

CHAPTER 9: FEEDING THE BEAST

THE NEXT MORNING...

HEY, BECK.

OH! HI!

UM...

THIS IS... A **LOT**.

WE HAVE TO BE **READY** FOR **EVERY** SCENARIO, DREW.

CONTAINMENT, LIKE... A **TRAP**?

YES, EXACTLY.

BUT I CAN'T FIGURE OUT HOW WE WOULD LURE HIM **INTO** IT.

HUH.

HE'S DRAWN TO YOUR EXTREME EMOTIONAL STATES, IS THAT RIGHT?

I **THINK** SO... LIKE WHEN I'M FEELING REALLY **BAD**.

INTERESTING. BUT NOT EXACTLY **RELIABLE**.

HE LIKES **DONUTS**, THOUGH. MAYBE WE COULD **LURE** HIM WITH **THOSE**?

DONUTS?

AND **LOTS** OF THINGS.

PRETTY MUCH **ANYTHING**.

BUT... WHERE DOES HE **FIND** DONUTS?

UMM...

...OR **DRAWINGS** OF DONUTS?

HAVE YOU BEEN **FEEDING HIM**, DREW!?

SHHHH!!

I MEAN...

I'VE BEEN MAKING **PROGRESS** WITH HIM...

DREW!!

191

UM...

SO...
THIS IS
WEIRD.

199

CHAPTER 10: ART CLUB UNITED?

SO...

I KNOW WHY YOU'RE HERE.

DREW...

LET ME SAY SOMETHING FIRST.

I HAVEN'T GIVEN YOU MUCH OF A REASON TO TRUST ME, BUT...

I WAS JUST TRYING TO MAKE THINGS RIGHT.

BECK TOLD US EVERYTHING, DREW.

IS IT TRUE?

LEVI...HE SHOULDN'T SUFFER FOR WHAT I DID.

I TRIED TO CROSS HIM OUT LIKE HE WAS JUST...SOME KIND OF MISTAKE.

RAR

RRP?

WHAT DID THEY JUST **DO?**

ZENOBIA?

WHAT'S **GOING ON?**

PLEASE WORK, **PLEASE...**

BUT...

HE...

YOU'RE **HURTING** HIM!

ARROOOUUC

RICKY'S RIGHT!

HE'S IN **AGONY!**

YOU'RE **TEARING HIM APART!**

IT'S A DIFFICULT PROCESS, DREW!

I DON'T **LIKE** IT, BUT...

UH-OH.

WHAT'S GOING ON?

THIS...
IT'S NOT
GONNA...

NONE OF
THIS IS
WORKING.

GRANDPA, LOOK!

LET'S HELP!

SURE! WHAT **IS** IT?

Chapter 11:
A New
Doodleville

OKAY, LEVI...

WE'VE PRACTICED THIS A **MILLION** TIMES.

BRING THE **HAT** BACK TO THE **BABY**, THEN GET **OUT** OF THERE!

JUST STICK TO THE PLAN... AND WE'RE **GOOD**.

TO BE
CONTINUED . . .

ACKNOWLEDGMENTS

I'm eternally thankful to everyone who helped me in countless ways over the course of *Doodleville*'s long journey. Although I can't possibly list everyone, I wanted to specifically thank:

My editor, Marisa DiNovis, for her endless support, enthusiasm, and unerring eye for detail. April Ward for her incredible art direction, and the entire Knopf team: Melanie Nolan, Josh Redlich, Brenda Conway, Janine Perez, Kristin Schulz, Jake Eldred, Nancy Siscoe, Artie Bennett, Alison Kolani, Emily DuVal, Nicole Valdez, Dawn Ryan, and Sylvia Bi.

My literary agent, Dan Lazar, for more than a decade of advice, advocacy, and encouragement.

Barbara Perez Marquez, Teo DuVall, Jasmine Walls, Deanna Arsala, Levi Hastings, David DeMeo, Michael Cole, Manuel Betancourt, Vid Alliger, Adam Guerino, Steve Foxe, Ingrid Law, and Mary Winn Heider, who gave crucially important feedback and encouragement.

The Art Institute of Chicago.

My parents, Tom and Pat.

My husband, Dan.

AUTHOR'S NOTE

Drawing can be magical.

I've been drawing my whole life, and it still feels like magic to me. Although my doodles don't dance across my walls or hide in priceless paintings, I'm able to bring them to life with my comics. After all, that's how I shared Drew's story with you in this very book!

Sometimes, though, drawing can be frustrating and a lot of work. It's taken me a long time to make *Doodleville*. Believe it or not, I first started working on this book more than ten years ago! And many of the characters you've met in *Doodleville* have been living in my head for even longer than that. (I'll share some more about them in the next few pages!)

I hope that reading this book inspires you to bring your *own* characters to life, whether in sketchbooks, in comics, or even on the walls of your home! (But maybe check with a grown-up first!)

And I hope that this book encourages you to *share* your characters and their stories, too! Art can connect us with each other. And it can communicate how we're really feeling. When you combine your creativity with the talents of others, you never know what might happen! My first graphic novel, *The Cardboard Kingdom*, was made with ten other writers. They helped me see my characters with fresh eyes, and they gave me the confidence to write and draw *Doodleville* by myself! Even when I doubted my abilities, they gave me the advice and the encouragement I needed to make this book.

Doubt is the enemy of every artist, young or old. It is what creates the Dark Leviathan and causes so much trouble for Drew and her friends. Draw fearlessly and don't fuss over flaws. Don't worry about erasing or crossing things out. Learn from your mistakes, but don't get *stuck* on them. The only way to get *better* at drawing is to *keep* drawing.

Like I said, I have spent ten years trying to tell Drew's story in *Doodleville*. Over the course of those years, I struggled with doubt and made mistakes, but I also learned a whole lot. Many friends helped me along the way by reading this book and sharing their feelings about it, whether good or bad. As I look back on it, ten years doesn't really seem so long, and every challenge along the way was a lesson I had to learn to make the book that you are holding in your hands right now.

In a way, Drew's story in *Doodleville* is a lot like my own—full of drawing and doubt and doodles. But it's just the start of *her* story! Drew's adventures will continue in Book 2 of the Doodleville series!

AN ANNOTATED HISTORY OF THE DOODLES

Some of the doodles that you've met in *Doodleville* can be found in the oldest sketchbooks from my own childhood! I went digging through dozens of those books to find their first few sketches and to share a little bit about how they've grown (or, in some cases, shrunk??) over the years!

PANJA

I first started drawing Panja when I was twelve or thirteen, and I haven't stopped drawing him since! He was originally going to be a ninja panda—that's where his name comes from! But over time, he's transformed into less of an action hero and more of an adorable little friend!

BILLY

I've been drawing Billy since I was a teenager. He's always been goofy and generous, expressive and innocent. I love the idea that a slug, which might be slimy and gross to some people, is actually a total sweetheart! No matter what, Billy tries to help his friends, even if he doesn't know how.

KITTYBUNNY

Kittybunny, a cute cat with floppy bunny ears, is the complete opposite of Billy the Slug—and she's got a dark side! In fact, you can see in this early sketch of her that I originally gave her demon horns instead of rabbit ears! But I don't think I meant to give her wheels—those circles were part of a different doodle! Oops!

MIKE

I've always thought of Mike as a big, friendly ogre. He's a little less fearsome nowadays than when he started out, though. Back then, he had bigger teeth and claws. At some point, he developed a fondness for hats, which was an unexpected (but delightful) surprise!

THE ART CLUB'S HEROES

CAPTAIN COCKATOO

I love superheroes, especially if they're based on silly animals. Much like Ameer, I had a bird as a pet when I was a kid. Though instead of his majestic pink cockatoo, I had an adorable little cockatiel!

(Yes, they're different kinds of birds!) Although I have drawn Captain Cockatoo in a lot of different ways over the years, my favorite part of drawing him has always been the tuft of feathers on top of his head because it is so funny, fluffy, and expressive!

DINAH DARE

I've always loved science fiction—whether I'm reading about space, or time travel, or futuristic technology! Dinah Dare is an inventor extraordinaire: anything you can think of, she can make it! But even though Dinah's gadgets are high-tech, I made them all really fun and easy to draw, often using simple shapes like circles and triangles.

BRU

I wanted each of the Art Club's characters to have a distinctive style, and with Bru, my design was all jagged angles and pointy bits—even that wand is crooked! When I was creating this character, I had someone in mind like Amethyst from *Steven Universe* meets Sam the Goblin from *The Cardboard Kingdom*!

THE MAGICAL BUTTERFLY BOYFRIENDS

The two princes were inspired by cartoons like *Sailor Moon*, which feature fabulous costumes, magical accessories, and lots of sparkles. Their magic is about connection, and they are more powerful when they are together. I like to think that real life is like that, too—that we're capable of achieving amazing things when we reach across our differences and connect with each other.

Many of the other doodles in this book are more recent creations, and they resulted from several long sessions of doodling and daydreaming just to see what would happen! Sometimes I would create a creature, and I wouldn't even know what they were supposed to be! That might seem strange, but it's what Drew does with her doodles, too. They rarely turn out the way she expected! The characters you draw today might grow and change alongside you all your life!

HOW TO DRAW A DOODLE

One of my favorite doodles to draw is Gloop. There's no wrong way to draw Gloop!

1. First, start with an eye—just a circle and a dot in the middle!

2. Second, draw another eye wherever you want.

3. His mouth looks kind of like a bean.

4. Give him two teeth!

5. Now draw a circular shape for his head.

6. Draw some more squiggles for his body! There you go! That's Gloop!

Doodleville is dedicated to the arts educators who made me the artist that I am, and to those who continue teaching their students to make magic every day in their classrooms.
—C.S.

THIS IS A BORZOI BOOK PUBLISHED BY ALFRED A. KNOPF

This is a work of fiction. Names, characters, places, and incidents either are the product of the author's imagination or are used fictitiously. Any resemblance to actual persons, living or dead, events, or locales is entirely coincidental. Except for the Art Institute of Chicago and Stan's Donuts. Those are real places. They just don't (usually) have doodles causing mischief in them.

Text and illustrations copyright © 2020 by Chad Sell

All rights reserved. Published in the United States by Alfred A. Knopf, an imprint of Random House Children's Books, a division of Penguin Random House LLC, New York.

Knopf, Borzoi Books, and the colophon are registered trademarks of Penguin Random House LLC.

Visit us on the Web! rhcbooks.com

Educators and librarians, for a variety of teaching tools, visit us at RHTeachersLibrarians.com

Library of Congress Cataloging-in-Publication Data is available upon request.
ISBN 978-1-9848-9470-0 (trade) — ISBN 978-0-593-12682-0 (lib. bdg.) —
ISBN 978-1-9848-9472-4 (ebook) — ISBN 978-1-9848-9471-7 (trade pbk.)

The text of this book is set in Creative Block BB.
The illustrations were created using Clip Studio Paint.
Interior design by Chad Sell

MANUFACTURED IN CHINA
June 2020
10 9 8 7 6 5 4 3 2 1

First Edition